OREGON

IDAHO

UTAH

NEVADA

Booooringest road in the world!

5

Nadia!

Sacramento

bear went over the mountain there and saw Yosemite (it fits the tune)

a ghost town right by this strange lake

580

80

210

Yosemite

Mono Lake

home of great neon signs

Grand Canyon

267

95

180

Las Vegas

93

64

still booooring

Sierra Nevada Mountains

395

HELLP!! California is about to fall into the ocean!

Mt. Whitney

Death Valley

I made it alive!

and I mean GRAND!

40

Manzanar

5

136

190

barbed wire - YUCCK!

40

cactus and more cactus

whale

why do they call this stretch of road the grapevine!? I didn't see any grapes

15

210

beep beep - lots of traffic

Los Angeles

CALIFORNIA

ARIZONA

PACIFIC OCEAN

sea monster

MEXICO

we didn't go here

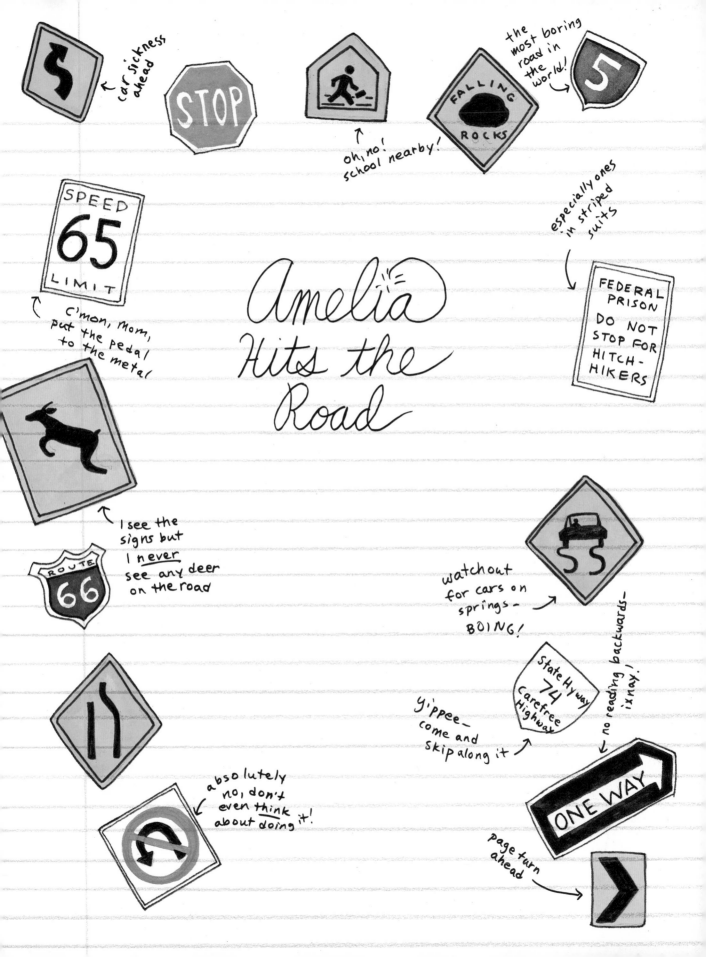

car sickness ahead

STOP

oh, no! school nearby!

FALLING ROCKS

the most boring road in the world!

5

especially ones in striped suits

FEDERAL PRISON DO NOT STOP FOR HITCH-HIKERS

SPEED 65 LIMIT

c'mon, Mom, put the pedal to the metal

*Amelia Hits the Road*

I see the signs but I never see any deer on the road

ROUTE 66

watch out for cars on springs— BOING!

State Hy way 74 Carefree Highway

no reading backwards— ixnay!

Y'ippee— come and skip along it

absolutely no, don't even think about doing it!

ONE WAY

page turn ahead

VACATION **SCHEDULE** !!

*stickers from exotic places*

*my bag's packed— I'm outta here!*

Name _Amelia_

Address _on the road!_

School _is out!_ No more homework, no more books, no more teachers' dirty looks!

*no tests! no cafeteria food! no P.E.!*

| FREE! ↓ Time | | Period 1 | Period 2 | Period 3 | Period 4 | Period 5 | Period 6 | Period 7 | Period 8 |
|---|---|---|---|---|---|---|---|---|---|
| | From | beginning | dawn | next | soup | door | A | HWY 5 | me |
| | To | end | dusk | nothing | nuts | door | Z | HWY 40 | Nadia |
| **Monday** | Subject | playing | doing nothing | reading comics | eating | sight-seeing | snacking | tv watching | being friends |
| | Room | hotel | car | rest stop | diner | sight being seen | car | motel | Nadia's |
| | Instructor | me | myself | I | me again | guess who? | yo! | yours truly | me and Nadia |
| **Tuesday** | Subject | | | | | | | | |
| | Room | | | | | | | | |
| | Instructor | | | | | | | | |
| **Wednesday** | Subject | | | | | | | | |
| | Room | | | | | | | | |
| | Instructor | | | | | | | | |
| **Thursday** | Subject | | | | | | | | |
| | Room | | | | | | | | |
| | Instructor | | | | | | | | |
| **Friday** | Subject | | | | | | | | |
| | Room | | | | | | | | |
| | Instructor | | | | | | | | |

Have you seen my other books? **AMELIA'S NOTEBOOK, AMELIA WRITES AGAIN, MY NOTEBOOK (with help from Amelia),** and **AMELIA TAKES COMMAND** are in bookstores and libraries. Hope you like them!

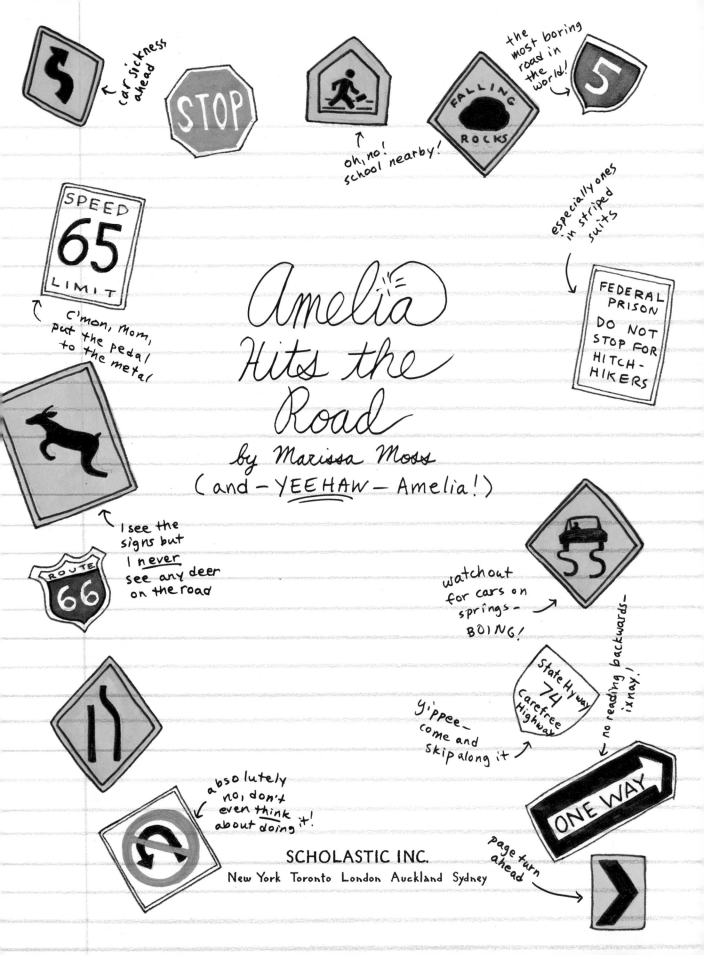

car sickness ahead

STOP

oh, no! school nearby!

FALLING ROCKS

the most boring road in the world! → 5

especially ones in striped suits

SPEED 65 LIMIT

c'mon, Mom, put the pedal to the metal

FEDERAL PRISON DO NOT STOP FOR HITCH-HIKERS

*Amelia Hits the Road*

by Marissa Moss

(and — YEEHAW — Amelia!)

I see the signs but I never see any deer on the road

ROUTE 66

watch out for cars on springs — BOING!

no reading backwards — ixnay!

State Hwy 74 Carefree Highway

Yippee — come and skip along it

ONE WAY

absolutely no, don't even think about doing it!

page turn ahead

SCHOLASTIC INC.
New York Toronto London Auckland Sydney

chapstick

floss
your teeth
(on vacation?)

← bug off stuff

ISBN 0-590-10833-6

yakkity shmakkity

this is
how many
bottles
of beer
on
the wall

Copyright © 1997 by Marissa Moss. All rights reserved.
Published by Scholastic Inc., 555 Broadway, New York, NY 10012,
by arrangement with Tricycle Press.
SCHOLASTIC and associated logos are trademarks and/or registered
trademarks of Scholastic Inc.

12  11  10  9  8  7  6  5  4                    9/9  0  1  2  3/0

Printed in the U.S.A.                              24

First Scholastic printing, June 1998

extra sock →

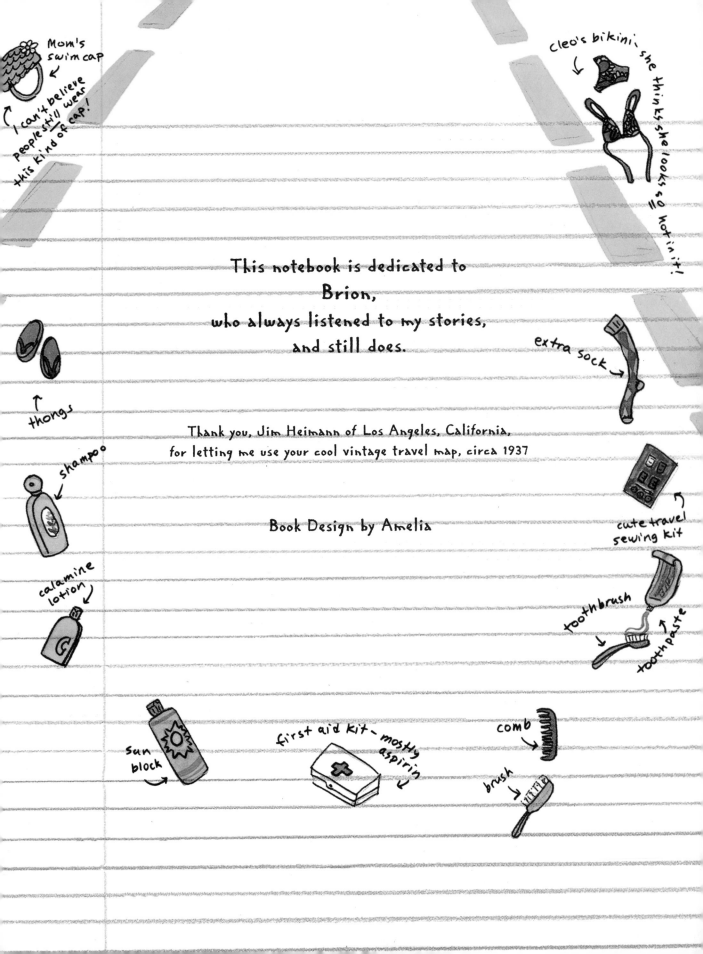

Mom's swim cap

I can't believe people still wear this kind of cap!

Cleo's bikini; she thinks she looks so hot in it!

This notebook is dedicated to
**Brion,**
who always listened to my stories,
and still does.

extra sock

thongs

shampoo

Thank you, Jim Heimann of Los Angeles, California,
for letting me use your cool vintage travel map, circa 1937

Book Design by Amelia

cute travel sewing kit

calamine lotion

toothbrush

toothpaste

sun block

first aid kit - mostly aspirin

comb

brush

ok to pass
this direction

no passing this direction

This is my new **TRAVEL** notebook. Mom bought it for me so I wouldn't be bored on the long driving part of this trip. She said if I'm busy writing, I won't be busy fighting with Cleo. I don't fight with Cleo. _she_ fights with me.

Mom also packed:

lots of small boxes of cereal for breakfast →

← good for snacks, too

a stack of shiny new comic books – _no_ schoolbooks, _no_ homework! nothing educational

gum to keep Cleo from getting carsick – I'm the only kid whose sister is world famous for throwing up in the car

← → bags in case the gum doesn't work – yuk!

Then of course we have the regular trip stuff:
calamine lotion, sunblock, bathing suits, clothes
(with extra socks – Mom believes you always need
extra socks, even in summer), shampoo, toothbrushes,
toothpaste, dental floss, and books, books, and
more books.

mom's box of paperbacks – she's panicked at the thought of being stuck anywhere without a book

Mom made me the navigator because Cleo can't read in the car without barfing

Cleo can't fold maps, either

I'm an expert folder of course

This is going to be a LOOOOOOONG trip. We're going to the Grand Canyon, Death Valley, and Yosemite. Then comes the best part — I get to see Nadia again! I mean, even though we moved, she's still my best friend. We've been friends since kindergarten, and that's a long time. Now it's been almost a year since I saw her. (Writing letters and talking on the phone is not the same as being with someone.) I hope she still likes me in person. I wonder if she looks the same or if she's changed.

Nadia — before

cool, shiny braces smile

eyes are happy to see me

hair this long

Nadia — now

is her hair short or long?

?  ?  ?

maybe she wears glasses now

same smile? is she happy to see me?

at least her ears must be the same

me →

have I changed? I don't think so. I haven't even grown an inch!

this was a tricky position to draw, especially since I need one hand to hold my nose because of the putrid, purple stink →

Oh, Baby, oh, marshmallow pie-ie ie-ie-ie-ie-ie! Oh, Baby, oh, spit in my eye-eye-eye-eye-eye-eye!

putrid purple

Cleo, painting her toenails and screeching out a song

Cleo crud →

Being stuck in a car with Cleo is NOT my idea of fun. She stinks up the car with the smell of nail polish. She BURPS so loudly Mom jumps a foot off her seat. She turns up the air conditioner so high my teeth start chattering. And she sings the stupidest songs ever— offkey, of course.

Mom says we should enjoy this togetherness. It seems like TOO much togetherness, if you ask me. Especially when Cleo gets carsick. Then the last thing in the world I want is to be together with her!

this car is definitely not big enough, we should put Cleo in a trailer behind the car

fumes-PU!

Cleo puking

all our junk piled up in back

me trying to get some fresh air

windows wide open

barf bags

mystery celebrity inside?

we also count cars, but only Bugs and limos score →

Today is the <u>longest</u> day of my life! Every minute takes about a year. Mom says it will be worth it once we get to the Grand Canyon. (But it will only be worth it if she pays me a million dollars!)

We've been playing the license plate game for hours (or decades!). By the time we get to the Grand Canyon, I bet I'll see <u>all</u> the states.

↑ our old home state

Last night Mom let me sit up front with her while Cleo snored in the back. Then it was cool to drive. I saw about a zillion stars, and the moon followed us. Even the roadside signs looked magical in the dark. I wish it could always
     be like that. (Especially the sleeping
        Cleo part.)

our new home state ↗

matchbook for my collection

sugar pack

Driving was still booooring today, but at least we ate dinner at a great diner. The pumpkin pie was good, but the best part was the jukebox. It was a real old-fashioned one, all lit up, and you could see the records (not CDs!) drop. Cleo put a quarter in, and we danced together. It was fun! There were some great songs Mom remembered from when she was a kid. She thinks music today is terrible— but then, she's a mom.

cake in a cake stand, like it's a jewel or something

metal napkin holder - just try to get one napkin

me and Cleo dancing- Cleo even dipped me!

jukebox

caw-fee pot

floor like a chessboard

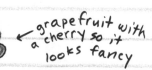
Jell-O cubes

grapefruit with a cherry so it looks fancy

thick mugs for hot chocolate with whipped cream on top

toilet gift wrap

In the motel, I couldn't stop laughing. Cleo kept on cracking me up. When she saw the paper strip they put on the toilet seat, she acted like it was a present wrapped up for her.

We opened all the drawers, tried all the TV channels, and inspected the closet. It was too late to go swimming in the pool, but the Bible in the nightstand drawer gave me a great idea — Cleo and I wrote funny notes to leave in all the dresser drawers.

A surprise for me? You shouldn't have! It's tooo much! At last, a place to throw up. No more bags for me.

wrapper

flusher

I guess Cleo doesn't like puking any more than I like seeing (and smelling) her puke

PU! Don't put stinky socks in this drawer!

Didn't your mother teach you to fold your clothes NEATLY!?

Did you flush the toilet? Did you wash your hands?

Beware of chewing gum left in drawers — yuuuch!

No eating chips in bed!

I wrote postcards to Nadia and Leah before I went to bed. Nadia says she's glad I met Leah and have a new friend, but I wonder, does that mean she has a new friend, too?

Here's what I wrote

FEENY'S MOTEL
Drive in and dive in!

Dear Leah,
This is the motel we're staying at tonight. I didn't get to swim in the pool because we got here too late, but no way I'm sitting in that hot, sticky (and stinky) car tomorrow unless I get to swim first! Yours till the hot dog st—

Leah Feinberg
2282 Lomo
Oopa, Oregon
97881

Hungry Hamburger
— Clean your plate!

Dear Nadia,
It feels great to be out of the car! So far the most interesting thing I've seen on this trip is the pool here. At least Cleo only threw up once today. (She's the Barf Queen!)

Nadia Kurz
61 South St.
Barton, CA
91010

yours till UDK,
Amelia
(P.S. I can't wait to see you!)

Drive in
and dive in

mouse trap

drain trap →   ↑ floor

trap door   tourist trap

corny roadside reptile zoo—2 lizards and 1 snake

I like staying in motels, I like eating in restaurants, but all this driving, driving, driving is driving me crazy! We sang every song we could think of —"Found a Peanut", "On Top of Old Smoky", "Down by the Banks of the Hanky Panky", "The Bear Went over the Mountain", "Goofy Grimy Gopher Guts"— until Mom screamed at us to

**STOP!**

Then Cleo started reading every sign we passed until I hit her to shut her up and she hit me back so I hit her again and Mom yelled at us some more.

I asked Mom if she was enjoying all this togetherness. She just glared at me.

> Eat at Joe's
> Passing Lane
> Ahead Ga—

So when we saw the billboard that said:

> **MYSTERIOUS PLACE**
> **30 MILES AHEAD**
> *Stop and Experience the Mystery!*

I begged Mom to stop. She said forget it, it's just a junky tourist trap. The next sign said:

me in high begging gear

MYSTERIOUS PLACE
15 MILES TO GO TO THIS
UNIQUE and AMAZING SIGHT

please please please please please please please please please please please pretty please with sugar and whipped cream and sprinkles and chocolate chips and a cherry on top — pleeeeeeeeeease!

I really begged. I needed to get out of that car!
I guess Mom did too, because when we came to the
next sign:

MYSTERIOUS PLACE
~ JUST 5 MILES AHEAD ~
DON'T MISS THIS INCREDIBLE SIGHT

she said, "Well, maybe we could use a break to
stretch our legs." And when we came to the last sign:

HERE IT IS!!
the Amazing, Incredible, Unique, Extraordinary
MYSTERIOUS PLACE
DON'T DRIVE BY OR YOU WILL REGRET
IT FOR THE REST OF YOUR LIFE!

she pulled in and stopped.

I'VE EXPERIENCED ????????? ? THE MYSTERIOUS PLACE

What we saw next was so astounding I'm not sure I can write about it. The Mysterious Place was — indescribable. At least, I can't describe it, but Mom's word for it was "cheesy"— and she didn't mean cheddar.

ball rolls UP hill— defying forces of gravity!

wooden slide built into hill

For this we paid $8 plus $1 for parking — what's mysterious is why anyone would give money to see this!

Some wonder! Really the slides are downhill. They just look uphill because of the slope of the ground and the path we were on. Duh!

Cleo, completely amazed — she has to take a picture of this wonder

Mom, completely disgusted

The truly mysterious place was the gift shop, where there was an astonishing display of junk. I couldn't believe anyone would buy that stuff. All I wanted was a soda, but Mom said she wasn't paying those high prices, and I didn't want to waste my own money.

They went to the MYSTERIOUS PLACE and all I got was this shirt

joke T-shirts

pom poms with feet and jiggly eyes glued to a magnet— oooh, how cute!

Genuine BUFFALO CHIPS

joke snacks

mystery caps

At least we got out of the car for a while.

Cleo wasted her money in the gift shop on some tarot cards — how mysterious!

When Cleo told my fortune with her new cards she said I would visit new places and meet new people. DUH! I knew that <u>without</u> a tarot deck. I wanted to tell her fortune, but she wouldn't let me touch her stupid cards. Anyway, I know what her fortune is: you will get a big pimple right on your nose, and everyone will stare at it.

magic eight ball — answers all questions

Cleo said I drooled when I fell asleep in the car. I DID NOT! But I did have a terrible dream. I was at Nadia's house, but when I opened the door, some other kid lived there. What a nightmare!

tea leaves — reveal the past, show the future

When I woke up, we weren't at Nadia's house, but we <u>were</u> at the Grand Canyon. Finally! Seeing it for real, not on TV or in pictures, was like a dream, a <u>good</u> one. I mean, it was familiar, but completely different, too.

First of all, it's . . . . . . . . . . . . . . . . . . . . .

palm reading — you hold your life in your hands

Ouija board — the spirit speaks!

Cleo believes in all this stuff — I'm not sure if I do or not kind of e sand castles, ut GIGANTIC ones!

← no dynamite, no special effects — just →
wind and the river made ALL THIS!

it's so orange
and red, it's
like being on Mars! ↑

# BIG!

It's so ENORMOUS it's like going to an
entirely different planet. As far as you can see, there
it is. And besides being HUGE, it is so old.
I felt like I was looking back in time, to prehistoric
earth. I mean, it took FOREVER for the river and
wind to make such deep channels. Mom says the
Grand Canyon is the Earth's old-age wrinkles, like
the lines on her forehead. (Nice try, Mom.)
   Cleo said it was just a big hole in the ground,
why bother to come, but I thought it was awesome!

(Cleo's favorite constellation—Hamburgerus)

and french fries (no ketchupus)

It was too late to hike, but the night was beautiful anyway. I've never seen so many stars in my <u>life</u>. I just sat outside our cabin and stared at the stars. It made me dizzy! Cleo showed me some constellations. I knew the Big Dipper and Orion before, but now I know Taurus and Gemini, too.

I can find the stars that make Gemini, but I can't see twins in this

I can see this picture pretty easily — except for the legs

constellations are like giant dot-to-dots, but once you connect the dots, you still have to imagine the picture

Orion →

Taurus is really hard to see, but its eye is really bright, so that's what I looked for

I love to think that people saw and named those same stars thousands of years ago! But Cleo said that the stars we see might not even be there anymore because they're <u>so</u> far away that it takes <u>years</u> for light to travel from that particular star to my eye. I mean, I could see a star now that's already novaed (is that a word? Should I say went nova? Blew up? Exploded? Imploded? Outploded?). I can't think about that — it's <u>too</u> ~~wierd~~ ~~weird~~ ~~wierd~~ ~~weird~~ ~~wierd~~ weird!

AGGH! I <u>HATE</u> this word!

looking down at the canyon made me dizzy— and looking up made me even dizzier!

We got up early to see the Grand Canyon at sunrise (a major accomplishment for Cleo). It was spectacular — all orange and pink and yellow.

I can't imagine being the first person who saw all this. Especially because the land coming up to the edge is just ordinary, and then suddenly there's this amazing THING.

← unsuspecting tourist

ordinary tree

ordinary grass

← that first step is a doozy!

After breakfast, we hiked down the Kaibob Trail to Cedar Ridge. It was already hot, hot, HOT, and Cleo was whining, whining, WHINING, so I went ahead to get away from her. But I couldn't get away from the mule poop. Lazy people ride mules up and down the trail, and they poop everywhere (the mules, not the people), so I had to dodge stinky plops constantly.

why don't they just tie bags to the mule's tail to catch all the poop?

↑ mule

mule plop obstacle course - ooops!

mule diaper

dust waiting to be kicked up ↑

before hike ←
← sparkling white tennies

after hike ↓
dusty pink tennies ↗

The good part was being <u>inside</u> the canyon — definitely cool (even though it was hot). And I met a boy. His name is Mako. We hiked together the whole way. Mako is from Japan, and he's really nice. Cleo acted like a jerk, of course, saying how cute Mako is. Maybe he's a little cute, but mostly he's just fun to talk to, and I'd rather hike with him than Cleo <u>any day.</u>

Mako said there's nothing like the Grand Canyon in Japan. He took lots of pictures to show his friends. He even took a picture of me!

friendly brown eyes ↘
nice smile →
Mako ↙
← shiny black hair
even his voice is nice ←

We traded addresses so we can be pen pals.

Mako showed me how to write his name in Japanese — it's hard to do — I hope I got it right →

this is how you write <u>my</u> name in Japanese — it's in a special alphabet for words that aren't Japanese — that's <u>so</u> cool!

↑ chain of gum wrappers Mako gave me — he's an expert at this — once he made a chain 4 feet long!

← I wanted to get dreamcatcher earrings like this so I could catch good dreams and keep out the bad ones, but Mom said they were too expensive and I don't have pierced ears anyway (well, not yet) — so Cleo bought them for her friend Gigi (lucky Gigi!)

Maybe someday he'll even visit me like I'm going to visit Nadia.

I wanted to get Nadia something special from the gift shop, and I found the perfect thing. It's a pair of dolls. Nadia can pick which one she wants, and I'll keep the other one. My doll will remind me of Nadia, and her doll will remind her of me!

← the dolls look like this

the tag on them looks like this

Certificate of Authenticity
Handmade by
Native Americans
Artist: _dilionlol_
Artist#: _113.697_

↑ Thanks, Artist # 113.697!

Leah's rocks look like these (but I'm keeping a few) ↓

For Leah I got some beautiful stones, shiny and all colors.

Mom said we only had time for one last look at the Grand Canyon. It was all purple and red with long shadows. Every time we look at it, it's different. I wonder what it will be like if I come back when I'm grown up. Less mule poop, I hope.

HOWDY FROM THE LAND OF THE GIANT CACTUS!

ARIZONA

ARIZ...

ARIZONA
The Grand Canyon
State

SAGUARO CACTUS
BLOSSOM STATE FLOWER

Grand Canyon

Dear Nadia,
    Things feel very old here—
like time has stopped and
nothing's changed. I wish it
was like this everywhere, but
I know it's not. I mean,
stuff changes all the time.
But here even the names
sound really old — like
Horsethief Road, Bloody Basin
Gulch, Dead Horse Ranch.

Nadia Kurz
61 South St.
Barton, CA.
91010
B TRU 2 ME

Grand Canyon

Dear Leah,
    Pretty cool picture, huh?
I've seen a lot of amazing
things. The Grand Canyon
is too big to describe,
you'll just have to come
see for yourself. It's so
ancient, they've even found
dinosaur bones near here,
but the only monster I
see is Cleo.   Yours till the comic strips,
                                    Amelia

Leah Feinberg
2282 Lomo
Oopa, Oregon
97881

2 Nice 2B 4got 10!

← I got postcards at
   the gift shop, too

Zoo Pals 12¢

FAMOUS GIRAFFES
GERALDINE

Heroes
in Books
Peter  12¢

← sarsparilla    ← old-fashioned candy jars with old-fashioned candy with funny-sounding names
← horehound drops

this pump has personality!

Every day on this trip it feels like we're going back in time. We stopped at a store that was also a gas station, and the pumps were old-fashioned and rounded. They reminded me of a cartoon where everyone wears gloves so they have sausage fingers. Hands look friendly and funny that way, and so did the gas pump, not like the blah gas pumps we have now.

Mom says sometimes when things change, they get worse, not better. But she's not always right. She only likes old music. And, besides, I've seen her high school pictures — talk about dorky clothes!

macrame purses

long hair parted in the middle for boys and girls

hip huggers, some with bell bottoms, some not

bell bottoms

platform shoes

a singer Mom used to like wore shoes with a goldfish in each heel — how did he feed them? what if they died? Your feet would smell like rotting fish — PU!

clunky peace necklaces with leather ropes

boy (or is it girl?)

girl (or is it boy?)

tumble-
weeds
a-tumblin'

We had a picnic at a ghost town. No one had lived there for a LOOOONG time. There used to be a silver mine, so people rushed there to get rich. When the silver ran out, they all left. The buildings looked like they were holding their breath, waiting for the people to come back. I thought I would find some treasure or old coins, but I didn't.

LUCY
DILL
She was
a dilly.

1848-1891

R.I.P.
Pa Guffy

He took to his
bed, and there
he stayed,
till in this grave,
he was laid.

Here lies
Silver Pete
With his
saddle
At his feet

~1886~

Crackshot
Ed
until he met
Straight Shot
Bill

← the cemetery behind the town had some interesting tombstones—
some even told stories

Cleo found a bone. She said it was from a dead miner. Mom said it was a chicken bone from someone's picnic, but Cleo's keeping that bone like it's something special. She's going to write Gigi about it, and when we get home, they'll use the Ouija board to discover the bone's true identity.

Cleo,
astonished
to find
her treasure
is trash →

↑ Cleo's discovery—
chicken bone or
finger bone?

CHICKEN
1234567890

Gigi,
astonished
← to find her
friend is a
fool

the board speaks the truth!

cactus holding a hot dog

cactus with a bumpy nose

cactus wearing a skirt

cactus with a hairdo

We drove past miles and miles of cactus and tumbleweed, but no skeletons or bones (except Cleo's find). I thought we'd see something, but it was just a lot of nothing.

in movies you always see bones bleaching in the desert

Finally, after I'd asked "Are we THERE yet?" at least a zillion times, we came to this big castle. It was like a mirage, but it was real. Mom stopped the car (yeah!) and said, "Welcome to Death Valley." I thought for sure we'd see skeletons in Death Valley, but all we saw was a grave.

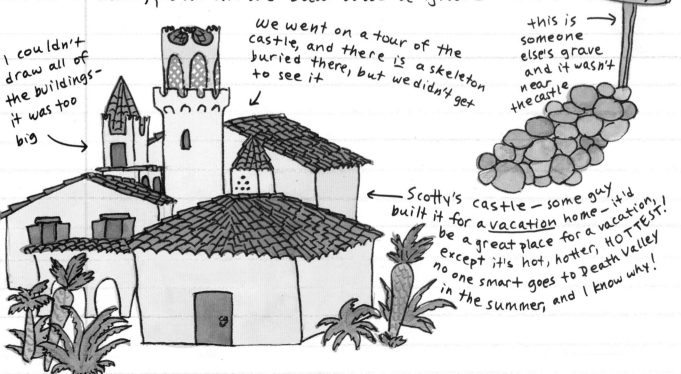

I couldn't draw all of the buildings— it was too big

we went on a tour of the castle, and there is a skeleton buried there, but we didn't get to see it

shorty

this is → someone else's grave and it wasn't near the castle

← Scotty's castle — some guy built it for a vacation home — it'd be a great place for a vacation, except it's hot, hotter, HOTTEST! no one smart goes to Death Valley in the summer, and I know why!

I didn't see this snake (phew!)— a sidewinder— but I saw its tracks all over the dunes

← squirrel prints

antelope squirrel— I saw one near Scotty's castle

this isn't a tiny kangaroo— it's a kangaroo rat — more tracks I saw in the sand dunes

snake footprints

tail print

It is really beautiful here. I just wish my clothes were air-conditioned. Near where we're staying there are miles and miles of sand dunes, but no beach. The waves of sand are like a dry frozen ocean. I would have built a sand castle, but I could only stand to be out of the car for 10 minutes before I felt like I was baking in a giant oven.

me surfing a sand wave

Then, in the middle of the desert, there's all this hard, dried-out salt, like there was once an ocean here. This place is so mixed up!

this raven really startled me — it had a sharp beak and glossy black feathers like a crow, but it was HUGE!

Cleo sprinkled some of that salt on her hard-boiled egg at our picnic lunch so she could say she'd eaten Death... Valley

rocks, sand, and more rocks and sand →

Badwater

↖ you aren't behaving, you *bad water*!

There are rocks and mountains, too. The best part is their names.

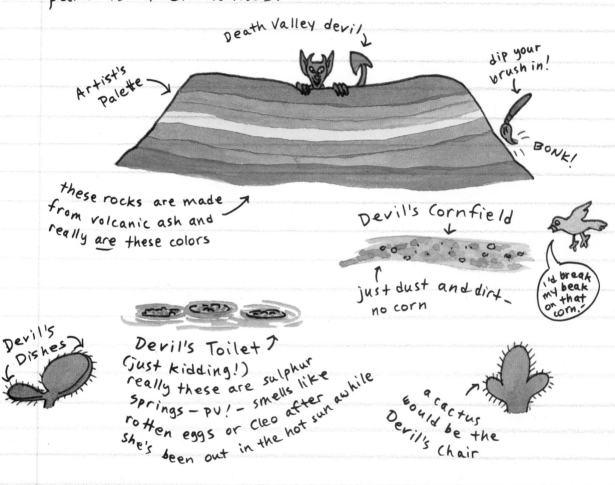

Death Valley devil ↓

Artist's Palette →

dip your brush in!

BONK!

these rocks are made from volcanic ash and really *are* these colors →

Devil's Cornfield ↓

just dust and dirt — no corn

I'd break my beak on that corn.

Devil's Dishes →

Devil's Toilet ↗ (just kidding!) really these are sulphur springs — PU! — smells like rotten eggs or Cleo after she's been out in the hot sun awhile

a cactus would be the Devil's chair

Mom says the desert is peaceful because it's so big and open. And quiet. I've never heard such LOUD quiet as here. Of course, Cleo says it's driving her crazy, but I like it. I wish Cleo would just stay in the hotel and paint her toenails if she's going to whine. All she does is drink soda and burp anyway. How can I hear the quiet with all her burping?

somebody's front yard— dirt and weeds

rusted out tractor— hasn't been used in a century

tall, tall weeds all around

old-fashioned silver trailer someone lives in — it looks like a spaceship

saggy crumbling sofa on saggy crumbling porch — come sit a spell!

for sale sign in window— wanna buy a bus?

petrified school bus

Outside of Death Valley, it still feels old and dusty and quiet. There are old mine shafts cut into the hills, and when we drive through towns, it's like no one lives in them. The yards are full of old rusting junk.

We hadn't gone very far when, even without me nagging, Mom stopped the car at one of those historical markers. It said we were in a place called Manzanar, where 10,000 Japanese-Americans lived during World War II. It was like a camp for war prisoners, only these people weren't enemy soldiers, just regular people — kids even! But since the U.S. was fighting Japan, our government thought even Japanese-Americans were bad. I can't believe a president could be so stupid. (I hope he got a lot of angry letters!)

i'm mad!

↑
barbed wire — it used to be all around the camp — it reminds me of when all the caution tape was up at school after the fire

I can't believe it really happened, but you can still see some guard posts and a cemetery with Japanese writing on the gravestones. Miss Know-It-All Cleo says she studied about Manzanar in social studies, but no one ever told me. I wonder if Mako knows.

I thought Mom would give us one of her "See how lucky you are" lectures, but she didn't.

all the rusted-out junk we passed seemed even sadder after Manzanar
↓

ancient broken swing set — when's the last time a kid had fun here?
↓

old pick-up truck that's so broken down it can't pick itself up and move
↓

dried-out weeds — even the weeds look old ↓

Cleo bought a little fan in Death Valley and now she won't leave the car without it — I hope it clips off the tip of her jelly roll nose!

We've seen a lot of strange things on this trip (besides Cleo in a bikini — gross!). Today we stopped at Mono Lake.

now this was a real Mysterious Place!

sand ooze

Mono Lake rock thing

bird poop

It has all these crumbly rock sculpture like formations. They look just like sand when you ooze it through your hands at the beach, only bigger (and harder). I wonder how all these different kinds of places get made.

This has been a great trip, except for two things — all the driving and Cleo! I've watched her paint her nails, sing off-key, throw up, chew food with her mouth open, burp, crack her knuckles, and pick her nose.

# I CAN'T STAND IT ANYMORE!

I couldn't help it. When Mom said it was time to get back in the car and head for Yosemite, Cleo started her usual whining chant.

I didn't yell. I didn't hit (though I wanted to do both). But I _did_ take my can of soda and I _did_ pour it over Cleo's head. Man, did that feel good!

Mom said no TV for me tonight at the motel, but it was _definitely_ worth it.

a new sugary-sweet hairdo ↓

Cleo after her soda shower →

same old sour personality

Cleo pouted all the way to Yosemite — too bad!

I wasn't sure our car would make it, because the road went up and up and up through the gray Sierra Mountains. If Cleo didn't eat all those hamburgers, the poor car wouldn't have to work so hard.

Then after all the grayness, we came out into Tuolumne Meadows, and we were in Yosemite! It was just like when Dorothy lands in Oz after being in black-and-white Kansas. It was amazing! Even Cleo couldn't stop smiling — the feeling of being someplace really special was so strong.

Cleo acting like she's in The Sound of music

I almost ran into a deer — it looked right at me

← lady using blow-dryer on her curlers while watching TV and blabbing

we got out of the car to run through this meadow full of wild flowers — the grass was so high, you could almost play hide-and-seek in it

Then we drove down into Yosemite Valley, past all these great rocks (I mean GREAT) and waterfalls. It was beautiful, but it definitely wasn't peaceful. It was CROWDED — people yakking, radios blaring, even TV sets blasting away from all the RVs.

bear warning sign - keep all food out of reach of bears

special trash cans to keep bears out

canned food-yum!

↑ bear looking for a snack

But once we started hiking above the Valley, we got away from the roller-bladers, the bikes, and the crowds. We still had Cleo, though.

this is the view from Glacier Point ↘

postcard from the valley store ↗

We hiked up Lambert Dome, and we could see ALL around for miles. I felt like I was floating on a cloud over all these mountains.

That was tasty, just like a hamburger. -BURP-

Cleo chanted "A million bottles of beer on the wall" on the hike back, but I just ran ahead so I wouldn't have to hear her. No way is she going to ruin Yosemite for me!
I hope a mountain lion eats her.

Bridalveil Fall— the water is <u>so</u> loud, it drowns out Cleo — great!

Half Dome — it looks like a scoop of ice cream (but it's not really pink)

we saw some people climbing this smooooth rock with ropes — it looked impossible, but they were doing it

Only a little more togetherness, and I'll be FREE of Cleo, at least for a little while. Tomorrow we go to Nadia's!

I'm excited, but I'm nervous, too. Will Nadia still like me? Or do I have a picture of her in my head that's not true anymore, like the stars I see but aren't really there? If I think about it too much, I'll get a stomachache.

BIG rock

tiny car

El Capitan— I salute you!

boy gets to fly all by himself

boy's house

grandparents' house

## The Visit

A boy visited his grandparents every year. They lived far away so he couldn't see them more than that. When they saw him, they always said, "Oh, you've grown so much! Look how you've changed!" But the boy felt exactly the same. Finally, one year, he noticed that <u>they</u> were the ones who were changing. His grandma had more white hair.

grandma's wrinkly prune face →

← wispy white hair

↘ boy.

← six hairs left

grandpa's old leathery face ←

His grandpa had almost <u>no</u> hair. And they both had lots more wrinkles. That scared him because he knew they were getting v<u>ery</u> old and could die any minute. That visit was the first time the boy felt he had changed, too, just like they said. He did feel older, but not better, just sadder. He hugged his grandparents very tight.

<u>That</u>'s not a good story. That's a <u>terrible</u> story! Am I worried that Nadia has wrinkles and is going to die? That is SO ridiculous! She's only TEN years old!

WATER    A Change for the Better    FOOD

A girl got a puppy for her birthday. She named him Tuffy T. Bone (or Tuffy for short). He was very cute, but also very wild. He pooped and peed everywhere. He chewed up her new shoes (and the rug and the chair and the curtains and the doormat).

← PUPPY POOP pile

PUPPY Pee puddle →

this was a shoe →

sharp puppy teeth →

this <u>was</u> homework ↓

He ate up her homework (and of course the teacher didn't believe her, even though she was telling the truth).

But, after a while, he got bigger. He wasn't as cute, but he didn't pee on the girl's things anymore, and he was a very good friend. He would go on walks and catch frisbees and curl up next to the girl when she did her homework. Sometimes she missed having a puppy, but mostly she loved having a dog.

this is not a UFO — it's a frisbee

wow! what a leap — a puppy couldn't do that! →

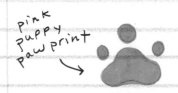

pink puppy paw print →

big dog paw print (still pink) ↓

← same store on the corner

← same newspaper rack

← same potholes in the street

↑ same plastic flamingos in the yard of the purple house (still purple)

Now that we're back in our old city, everything looks so familiar. Our old neighborhood, even our old house, is exactly the same, only it's not home anymore. When we parked in Nadia's driveway, I was **SO** nervous my hands were all sweaty.

our ex-home ↓

↑ the same as when we lived here, except there's a tricycle in the front yard — another kid must live here now

↑ same old lowing doorbell

I rang the doorbell and it seemed like forever but at last she opened the door — the same old Nadia with her same old smile, only NO BRACES!

She said, "Surprise! Now you see the real me." We looked at each other grin, grin, grinning, and then we hugged. It felt great!

same gingery shampoo smell

Nadia now ↓

no haircut ↘

still no glasses

same happy-to-see-me smile, but no more zipper teeth

another change — she got her ears pierced, she even owns 4 pairs of earrings!

wearing the necklace I made for her

Nadia put the doll on her shelf with all her special stuff

giant seashell her grandma gave her

blown glass animal collection

jewelry box with little lock and key

miniature books collection

pretty rock

I let her pick which doll she wanted. She picked the girl, and she's going to name her Amelia=! I can tell she really likes it, but next time, I'm getting her earrings.

And she had a present for me — it was a notebook of all the stories she's written. I can't wait to read them

the first story is called "Best Friends"

Nadia's notebook (now it's my notebook to read, not to write)

Nadia's room is just the way I remembered, except she has new drawings tacked to her bulletin board, the postcards I sent her — and a certificate with a ribbon for winning the Young Authors' Faire!

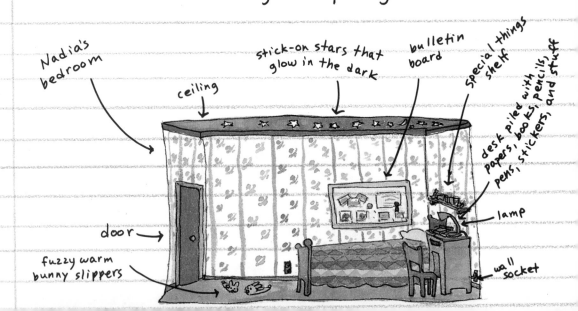

Nadia's bedroom

ceiling

stick-on stars that glow in the dark

bulletin board

special things shelf

desk piled with papers, books, pencils, pens, stickers, and stuff

lamp

door

fuzzy warm bunny slippers

wall socket

postcards from me

old school photo of me →

Young Authors' Faire
_Nadia Kury_
has been awarded
First Place
for excellence in writing

authors' faire certificate

blue ribbon

COUNT DOWN TO AMELIA
10 9 8 7
6 5 4 3
2 1 A

MAP OF A'S ROUTE

new drawings

Nadia's bulletin board

notes Nadia writes to herself to remind her of important things — like _my_ visit!

I asked her why she hadn't told me that she won, and she turned all pink (I forgot how pink she gets when she blushes). She said she didn't want me to feel bad because I hadn't won. But I didn't feel at all bad. In fact, I felt great! Nadia is a true friend to think of my feelings first, and I'm not jealous — well, maybe a little, but only of her earrings, not of her winning the Young Authors' Faire.

Nadia's earrings — one set looks like cute little grapes →

one set is a tiny pair of dice

I felt even better when she pulled out the Experiment Kit I sent her for her birthday. She saved it to do with me, just like she said she would!

But then she asked if <u>I</u> still wanted to do it with her. I said of course I do, why wouldn't I? And she said she thought <u>I</u> might have changed and maybe I wasn't interested in science anymore.

test tubes

test tube holder →

poisonous chemical— watch out!

some-thing oxide

chrom-ium dadada

Boric ladi-da

Sodium some-thing

← chemicals →

↑ tongs to hold test tube with

funnel

measuring beaker

little metal ↑ spoon to measure chemicals with

instruction booklet so you can make your own Frankenstein monster →

beaker

litmus paper →

simple experiment #1: Take a paper cup. Cut a hole in the bottom. Turn upside down and seal opening (<u>not</u> hole) with foil. Put a <u>big</u> spoonful of baking soda in the foiled bottom of the cup. In a beaker, mix vinegar (maybe half a cup) with red food coloring. Pour the mixture into the foiled cup. Watch it froth over — it's a volcano!

hole

cup →

baking soda goes in here first, then colored vinegar

← volcanic eruption

foil wrapped around cup

plate to catch lava flow

So all this time I had been worrying about Nadia changing, and she was thinking the same thing about me. But I haven't changed at all—no pierced ears, no new smile, nothing. But I asked Nadia, anyway, if she thought I'd changed.

And she said YES!

I couldn't believe it. How? How? How? I had to know!

At first she wouldn't answer me. Then she said, "I don't know. It's just that first you moved away and met all these new people, and I stayed here. Then you went on this great trip and saw all kinds of cool stuff, and I haven't gone anywhere. You have to tell me everything!"

wide open spaces

wide open road

Death Valley

Mako

Grand Canyon

Mysterious Place

Manzanar

Mono Lake

Yosemite

me

Dancing with Cleo

She's right!  I _have_ changed.

   And I _did_ have a lot to tell her.  I said it was going to be like the last time I slept over, when we talked till 4 in the morning.
   "Yeah," said Nadia. "_Some_ things never change."

   She was right again.

# USEFUL INFORMATION

*if this were really useful, it would tell me how to change Cleo*

*as in 24-hour service— room service, send up a pizza, please!*

*that's all I can take of sitting in the car!*

### Table of Time Measure

| | |
|---|---|
| 60 seconds | = 1 minute |
| 60 minutes | = 1 hour |
| 24 hours | = 1 day |
| 7 days | = 1 week |
| 30 days | = 1 calendar month |
| 12 months | = 1 year |
| 365 days | = 1 common year |
| 100 years | = 1 century |

*add them all together and you still don't get the Grand Canyon— you need eons for that*

### Table of Dry Measure

| | |
|---|---|
| 2 pints (pt.) | = 1 quart (qt.) |
| 8 quarts | = 1 peck (pk.) |
| 4 pecks | = 1 bushel (bu.) |
| 1 cord | = 128 cu. ft. |

*is this the grain of salt you take the Mysterious Place with?*

### Table of Liquid Measure

| | |
|---|---|
| 4 gills (gi.) | = 1 pint (pt.) |
| 2 pints | = 1 quart (qt.) |
| 4 quarts | = 1 gallon (gal.) |
| 31½ gallons | = 1 barrel (bbl.) |
| 2 barrels | = hogshead (hhd.) |

*OINK!*

### Table of Paper Measure

| | |
|---|---|
| 24 sheets | = 1 quire |
| 20 quires | = 1 ream |
| 10 reams | = 1 bale |

### Table of Linear Measure

| | |
|---|---|
| 12 inches | = 1 foot |
| 3 feet | = 1 yard |
| 16½ ft. (5½ yds.) | = 1 rod |
| 660 feet | = 1 furlong |
| 320 rods (5280 ft.) | = 1 mile |

*can you measure how people change? is there a table of people progress? is change always progress, anyway?*

### Miscellaneous Measures

| | |
|---|---|
| 12 units | = 1 dozen |
| 12 dozen | = 1 gross |
| 12 gross | = 1 great gross |
| 20 units | = 1 score |
| 1 hand | = 4 inches |
| 1 fathom | = 6 feet |
| 1 knot | = 6086 feet |
| 3 knots | = 1 league |
| 1 bu. potatoes | = 60 pounds |

*I can't fathom what a great gross Cleo is*

*all the mule poop on the Kaibob Trail*

*bowling, softball? soccer, or out of my?*

### Table of Cubic Measure

| | |
|---|---|
| 1728 cubic inches | = 1 cubic foot |
| 27 cubic feet | = 1 cubic yard |
| 128 cubic feet | = 1 cord of wood |
| 24¾ cubic feet | = 1 perch of stone |

Note: A cord of wood is a pile 8 feet long, 4 feet wide and 4 feet high. A perch of stone or brick is 16½ feet long, 1½ feet wide, and 1 foot high.

*feet made of ice cubes? BRRR — I wish I had these in Death Valley*

*don't mention the carpet*

### Table of Avoirdupois Weight

| | |
|---|---|
| 16 drams | = 1 ounce (oz.) |
| 16 ounces | = 1 pound (lb.) |
| 100 pounds | = 1 hundredweight (cwt.) |
| 2000 pounds | = 1 ton (T.) |
| 2240 pounds | = 1 long ton (LT.) |

### Table of Troy Weight

| | |
|---|---|
| 24 grains (gr.) | = 1 pennyweight (dwt.) |
| 20 pennyweights | = 1 ounce (oz.) |
| 12 ounces | = 1 pound (lb.) |

*a long ton of Cleo*

### Table of Circular Measure

| | |
|---|---|
| 60 seconds (") | = 1 minute (') |
| 60 minutes | = 1 degree (°) |
| 360 degrees | = 1 circumference |

Note: A degree of the earth's surface or a meridian = 69.16 miles at the equator

*I couldn't degree more*

### Table of Apothecaries' Weight

| | |
|---|---|
| 20 grain (gr.) | = 1 scruple |
| 3 scruples | = 1 dram |
| 8 drams | = 1 ounce |
| 12 ounces | = 1 pound |

*frankly, Scarlett, I don't give a dram!*

### Table of Surface Measure

| | |
|---|---|
| 144 sq. in. | = 1 sq. ft. |
| 9 sq. ft. | = 1 sq. yd. |
| 30¼ sq. yds. | = 1 sq. rod |
| 160 sq. rods | = 1 acre |
| 640 acres | = 1 sq. mile |

Note: An acre measures 208.71 on each side. A section of land is 1 sq. mile. A quarter section is 160 acres. A township is 36 sq. miles.

*how far apart can friends be and still be friends? an acre? a town? a state? a state of mind?*